ANIMAL ANTICS A TO Z

Tessa Tiger's Temper Tantrums

by Barbara deRubertis • illustrated by R.W. Alley

THE KANE PRESS / NEW YORK

Alpha Betty's Class

Alexander Anteater

Bobby Baboon

Corky Cub

Dilly Dog

Eddie Elephant

Frances Frog

Gertie Gorilla

Hanna Hippo

Izzy Impala

Jeremy Jackrabbit

Kylie Kangaroo

Lana Llama

Maxwell Moose

Nina Nandu

Oliver Otter

Polly Porcupine

Quentin Quokka

Rosie Raccoon

Sammy Skunk

Tessa Tiger

STAR
of the
BOOK

Umma Ungka

Victor Vicuna

Walter Warthog

Xavier Ox

Yoko Yak

Zachary Zebra

Alpha Betty

Library of Congress Cataloging-in-Publication Data

deRubertis, Barbara.
Tessa Tiger's temper tantrums / by Barbara deRubertis ; illustrated by R.W. Alley.
p. cm. — (Animal antics A to Z)
Summary: Tessa Tiger has terrible temper tantrums when her team loses at T-ball.
ISBN 978-1-57565-353-2 (library binding : alk. paper) — ISBN 978-1-57565-345-7 (pbk. : alk. paper) —
ISBN 978-1-57565-384-6 (e-book)
[1. Sportsmanship—Fiction. 2. Behavior—Fiction. 3. Tiger—Fiction. 4. Animals—Fiction.
5. Alphabet.] I. Alley, R. W. (Robert W.), ill. II. Title.
PZ7.D4475Te 2011
[E]—dc22   2010051318

1 3 5 7 9 10 8 6 4 2

First published in the United States of America in 2011 by Kane Press, Inc.
Printed in the United States of America
WOZ0711

Series Editor: Juliana Hanford
Book Design: Edward Miller

Animal Antics A to Z is a registered trademark of Kane Press, Inc.

www.kanepress.com

Tessa Tiger was very good at playing sports.

But she was NOT a very good sport.

5

Most of all, Tessa liked to play T-ball.

In fact, ALL the students in Alpha Betty's class
liked to play T-ball after school.
They had split their class into two teams.

Sometimes Tessa's team won.

Then Tessa would throw her hat in the air.
She would twist and twirl.
And she would hoot and holler.

Sometimes Tessa's team lost.

Then Tessa would hit her hat against a tree.
She would stomp and storm.
And once, she even stuck out her tongue!

"Stop, Tessa! Don't do that!" her team told her.

They were becoming more and more upset with Tessa.

One afternoon, the T-ball game was especially
exciting. The score was tied, 3 to 3.
There was one more inning.

Tessa's team was first to bat.
But no one scored a run.
Tessa's face looked stormy!

Then it was the other team's turn to bat.
And their first batter hit a home run!

Tessa's team had lost the game.

Tessa Tiger threw her most terrible temper tantrum EVER!

She tossed her mitt into a tree.
She kicked a basket of balls and stubbed her toe.
Then she tripped on a bat and fell.

Tessa tumbled topsy-turvy to the bottom of a hill.
And there she sat, crying buckets of tears.

Both teams rushed to help Tessa.
"Are you hurt?" they asked.

"NOOOOO!" screamed Tessa.
"T-ball is STUPID!"

All the kids put their hands over
their ears. They tiptoed away.

Tessa trudged home. She felt terrible.
Her mitt was lost. Her shirt was torn.
Her toe hurt. And, worst of all, she had a
temper-tantrum tummy ache.

The next morning, Tessa's team talked with their teacher, Alpha Betty. They told her about Tessa's terrible temper tantrum.

"Tessa's not a good sport," they said.
"She takes the fun out of playing T-ball.
We don't want Tessa on our team."

Tessa's team didn't know that she was just around the corner . . . *listening*!

17

Alpha Betty sat quietly for a minute.

She tapped her toes. She twiddled her thumbs.

She thought things over.

Then she smiled. "I have an idea."

Later that day, Alpha Betty made her class their
favorite treat—peanut butter on toast.

While they ate, she told a funny story.
It was about the time SHE threw a temper tantrum
when she was just a little lion cub.

"I had painted a picture of my twin sister,"
Alpha Betty told the class. "I had painted it
on the tablecloth . . . with *ketchup*!
It was a great artistic masterpiece.
But my sister washed it out!"

"I was SO angry with her," said Alpha Betty.
"I threw a real fit! Talk about temper tantrums!
I tossed around so much, do you know what
happened?" She paused.
"I twisted my own tail into a KNOT!"

All the students gasped!
But the thought of Alpha Betty having a temper
tantrum was just TOO funny!

The students were tickled. They started to giggle.
And they giggled until their tummies hurt—
in a good way!

Then Alpha Betty asked a question.
"Do you think temper tantrums are helpful?"

Tessa blurted out, "No!"

After that, words tumbled out of Tessa's mouth.

"Temper tantrums hurt your tummy in a BAD way.
And your friends don't want to play with you
anymore . . . ever again . . . in their whole lives."

Two big tears trickled down Tessa's face.

"What can you do instead of losing your temper?"
Alpha Betty asked the class.

Her students had lots of ideas.
"Stop and think before you blow up!"
"Try to make games FUN . . . for everyone!"
"Always be a good sport, win or lose!"

Tessa listened quietly.

Then, very softly, she spoke.
"I'm sorry about yesterday.
I'll be a better sport from now on.
Honest."

"That's great, Tessa!" her friends said.
"Do you want to play T-ball after school?"

Tessa smiled. "You BET!"

Tessa Tiger's team lost again that day.
Everyone turned to look at Tessa.
What would she do?

Well . . .

29

Tessa did NOT have a temper tantrum!

"Maybe we'll do better tomorrow," she grinned.
"And . . . maybe we won't! But win or lose,
there will be no knots in OUR tails!"

Then Tessa started to giggle. . . .

And Tessa Tiger and both teams laughed
until their tummies hurt—in a GOOD way!

FUN FACTS

- Home: Tigers live throughout Asia, in forests, grasslands, and swamps. The tiger is an endangered species, which means there are not many left on Earth.
- Size: Tigers are the largest members of the cat family. They are usually about 7 feet long, not including a 3-foot tail. They can weigh as much as 650 pounds!
- Appearance: The tiger has an orange-yellow coat that can have over 100 black stripes. But every tiger's stripes are a little different.
- Grrrrr: A tiger's roar can be heard from two miles away!
- **Did You Know?** Tigers are good swimmers, but they are not very good climbers! They climb trees only in emergencies.

LOOK BACK

Learning to identify letter sounds (phonemes) at the beginning, middle, and end of words is called "phonemic awareness."

- The word *tiger* <u>begins</u> with the *t* sound. Listen to the words on page 15 being read again. When you hear a word that <u>begins</u> with the *t* sound, make a "t" with your pointer fingers and say "*t-t-t*"!
- The word *pat* <u>ends</u> with the *t* sound. Listen to the words on page 7 being read again. When you hear a word that <u>ends</u> with the *t* sound, pat the top of your head and say "*t-t-t*"!
- **Challenge**: The word *batter* has the *t* sound in the <u>middle</u>. Change the first letter (*b*) to *m*. What word have you made? Now change the first letter to *p*, and then to *t*.

TRY THIS!

Sit on a chair and listen carefully as each word in the word bank below is read aloud slowly.

- If the word <u>begins</u> with the *t* sound, touch your **toes**!
- If the word <u>begins</u> with the *st* sound, **<u>stand</u>** up . . . and then sit down again!

tap stomp tree storm team
stick tumble toss stub stream
story tummy stumble stoop trip
toss star toe stop

FOR MORE ACTIVITIES, go to Tessa Tiger's website: www.kanepress.com/AnimalAntics/TessaTiger.html
You'll also find a recipe for Tessa Tiger's Tasty Taco Dip!

32